3 1160 00094 0747

BLOOMFIELD TWP. PUBLIC LIBRARY
MICHIGAN

THE HIDING GAME

story and pictures by Ben Shecter

Parents' Magazine Press
New York

Copyright © 1977 by Ben Shecter
All rights reserved
Printed in the United States of America

Library of Congress Cataloging in Publication Data
Shecter, Ben.
    The hiding game.

    SUMMARY: Two friends decide that playing hide
and seek isn't as much fun as doing things
together.
    [1. Friendship—Fiction. 2. Hide-and-seek—
Fiction] I. Title.
PZ7.S5382Hi [E] 76-18137
ISBN 0-8193-0856-0 ISBN 0-8193-0857-9 lib. bdg.

For Jennifer

AUG 1 8 1977 B. & TAYLOR

1

Rain forests make good hiding places.
Henri hippopotamus hid in a tree. And when Pierre
rhinoceros came looking for him, he said, "You can't
find me. I'm hiding."
"Hiding from what?" asked Pierre.
"Hiding from you!" answered Henri.
"Well, you can't be hiding from me if I know where
you are," said Pierre.

"That's true," said Henri, and he came down from the tree. "Close your eyes, then, and I'll hide someplace else." Pierre closed his eyes and Henri ran off. He hid in the vines that grew alongside his house.

"You can open your eyes," shouted Henri. "Now find me!" Pierre opened his eyes and walked directly to where Henri was hiding.
"How did you know I was here?" asked Henri.

"I heard you," Pierre said.

"All right, this time close your eyes and count to
one hundred," said Henri. "Then I won't have to say
anything."

Once again Pierre closed his eyes. Henri ran off into the coconut grove. He hid in a pile of coconut husks. "This is a perfect hiding place," he told himself.

2

When Pierre opened his eyes, he shouted, "I'll find
you, Henri!"
Pierre looked inside Henri's house and out. He searched
through rows of bushes and up the big-leafed banana tree.
He ran to the fields calling, "Henri hippopotamus,
Henri hippopotamus, I'll find you!"

But all he found was Lion asleep, Ostrich
nesting, and Hyena munching on some old bones.
He asked Hyena if he had seen Henri hippopotamus.

Hyena said he hadn't, but he invited Pierre to share
a snack with him.
Pierre said, "No thank you, old bones make me thirsty."
He kept on looking for Henri.

His search took him to the village, where he met
Chicken and her friends.
"Hello, Chicken," said Pierre. "I'm looking for Henri
hippopotamus. Have you seen him?"

"No," Chicken said. "But if we do I'll tell him that
you're looking for him."
"He already knows that," said Pierre, and he went on
his way.

3

The day grew warm. Pierre walked to the river. There Snake and Crocodile were swimming.

"Come join us," they shouted when they saw him.

"I'd like to," said Pierre, "but I'm busy looking for Henri hippopotamus."

"Is he lost?" they asked.

"No, we're just playing."

"Then come into the water and play with us for a while," Snake suggested.

Pierre looked at the cool water. "Okay!" he said, and jumped in.

Then Pierre cried, "Help! I don't know how to swim!"
Snake and Crocodile held Pierre. "We'll teach you,"
they offered.
It didn't take long for Pierre to learn to swim, and to
float. After a while he was truly enjoying himself in
the river.

Meanwhile Henri was getting tired of waiting for
Pierre. The termites that lived in the coconut pile
were also making him uncomfortable.

So Henri left his hiding place and began to look for
Pierre. He went searching through the fields and
the village.

In town, he asked if Pig had seen Pierre rhinoceros.
Pig said he hadn't and, furthermore, he was glad of it.
"The last time I saw Pierre we had a quarrel," said Pig.
"He chased me, and I couldn't catch my breath or eat a
thing for hours. It was awful. I lost five pounds."
Henri said he was sorry to hear about Pig's troubles
and left the village.

After looking everywhere but the river, Henri
gave up. He went to Pierre's house to wait
for his friend. And there he fell asleep on Pierre's
bed.

By now the sun had set and the moon rose in its
place. Pierre was tired of swimming. He thanked Snake
and Crocodile for the lesson, and set off for home. He
arrived with the first morning light.

"Henri hippopotamus, I've found you!" shouted Pierre.
Surprised by Pierre's sudden appearance, Henri woke up.
"Yes, you finally found me," he yawned.

"Tomorrow, let's play again," said Pierre. "Only
next time I'll hide and you can look for me."
"It already is tomorrow," said Henri. "And besides,
I played that way yesterday!"

"You did?" Pierre asked.

Henri nodded. "When you didn't find me, I began looking for you." And while the two friends were eating breakfast, Henri told how he had left his itchy hiding place to search for Pierre.

They both laughed.

"I have a better idea for us today," said Pierre.

"Let's go swimming."

"I love to swim!" said Henri.
So that's exactly what they did.
And it was a lot more fun being together than
spending the whole day looking for each other!

Ben Shecter, *a well-known illustrator and author of many children's books, began his career as a theatrical set designer. This background holds him in good stead when it comes to creating convincing color-splashed locales for his own tales. In* The Hiding Game, *the artist fulfilled a wish "to write a story that was different—something set outside my usual woodland scenery." A longtime resident of New York City, Mr. Shecter now lives in an old stone house in upstate New York.*